Illustrations by Benny Rahdiana

Printed in the United States of America
First Printing, 2020
ISBN 978-0-9771630-2-1
TTL,LLC
Throwback Publishing Company

www.theellerays.com
Instagram: @theellerays

CHAPTER 1:
OUT OF THIS WORLD

Have you ever seen real magic
That took you to another time and space?
Well, sisters Ari, Bri, and Little Lily
Discovered such a special place.

Their simple act of falling asleep
Would unlock mystical powers
That would take them on a fantastic journey
Of hidden inner jewels upon the world
they would flower.

It all began one day after school
When the sisters came home energetic.
They ran, and played, and bounced, and jumped
Until Ari said, "Mommy, your phone is ringing.
You should get it."

Surprised, Mommy stopped stirring the dinner
To see if she, too, could hear the sound
But all she heard were the sounds of the sisters
Playfully running around.

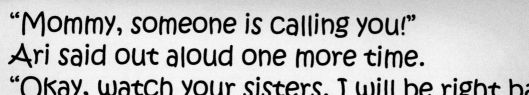

"Mommy, someone is calling you!"
Ari said out aloud one more time.
"Okay, watch your sisters. I will be right back,"
Mommy said
And made her way toward the stairs to climb.

When she got to her room,
Mommy was shocked to see
That she indeed had several missed calls.
But her phone was set to vibrate
So how could Ari have heard it at all?

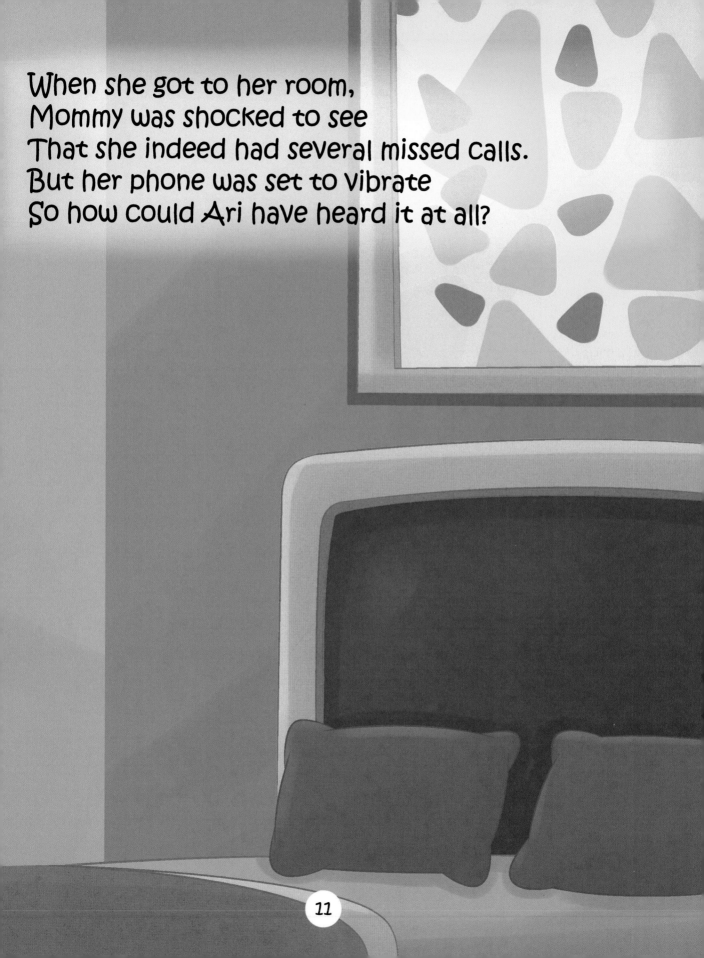

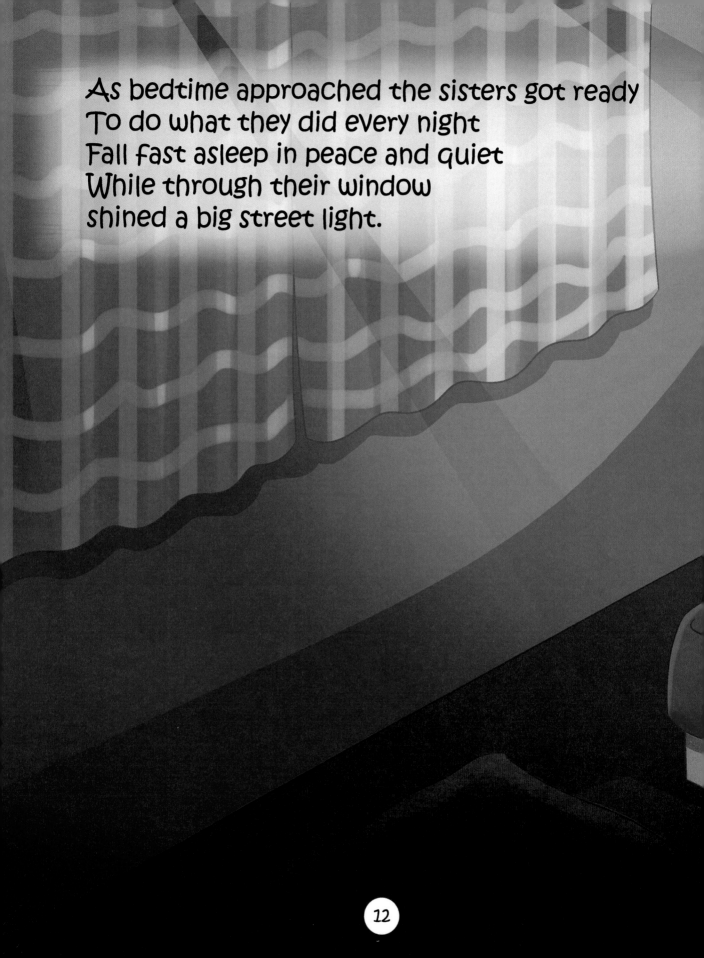

As bedtime approached the sisters got ready
To do what they did every night
Fall fast asleep in peace and quiet
While through their window
shined a big street light.

But this night was surprisingly darker than before
And this frightened Little Lily the most.
So Ari and Bri told her to hold their hands
For no way would they let anything close.

As they connected their hands and
drifted off to sleep
Everything around them was suddenly bright
Big gold triangles danced around them
It was such a wonderful sight.

Then suddenly, a huge explosion
Sent the sisters flying into the air
Through the trees and the clouds
they soared like birds
Where they were going? They were unaware.

16

As they flew far into the galaxy
They were suddenly hit by three rays
A red, a purple, and a pink ray of light
Brightly guided their way.

Ari drifted on a red ray of strength
And felt stronger than she ever had before
Bri was purple, and Little Lily was pink
Showing wisdom and beauty
that couldn't be ignored.

They returned to the earth with hands aglow
In each of their brand new colors.
Ari spotted their house from above the clouds
And led the sisters back to their bed and covers.

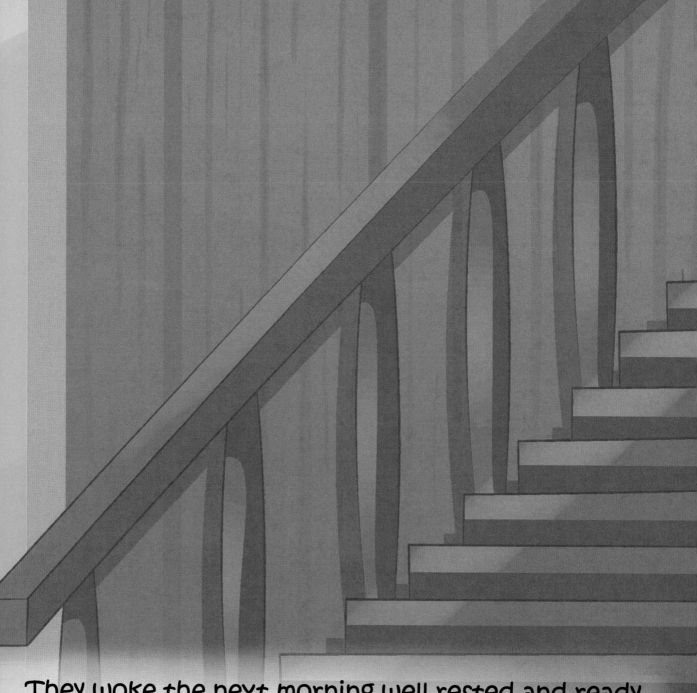

They woke the next morning well rested and ready
To take on another school day
Ari told Mommy about the dream she had
And Bri told her dream the same way.

Mommy thought it was a coincidence
That the two sisters shared the same dream
Little Lily was too young to tell her own story
But she knew everything she had seen.

The three sisters gathered their books for school
And piled all together in their van
Mommy dropped the sisters off
Before the school day officially began.

While at her locker putting away her books
Ari's friend Leanne came running over
She was smiling from ear to ear with excitement
Because Leanne had something to show her.

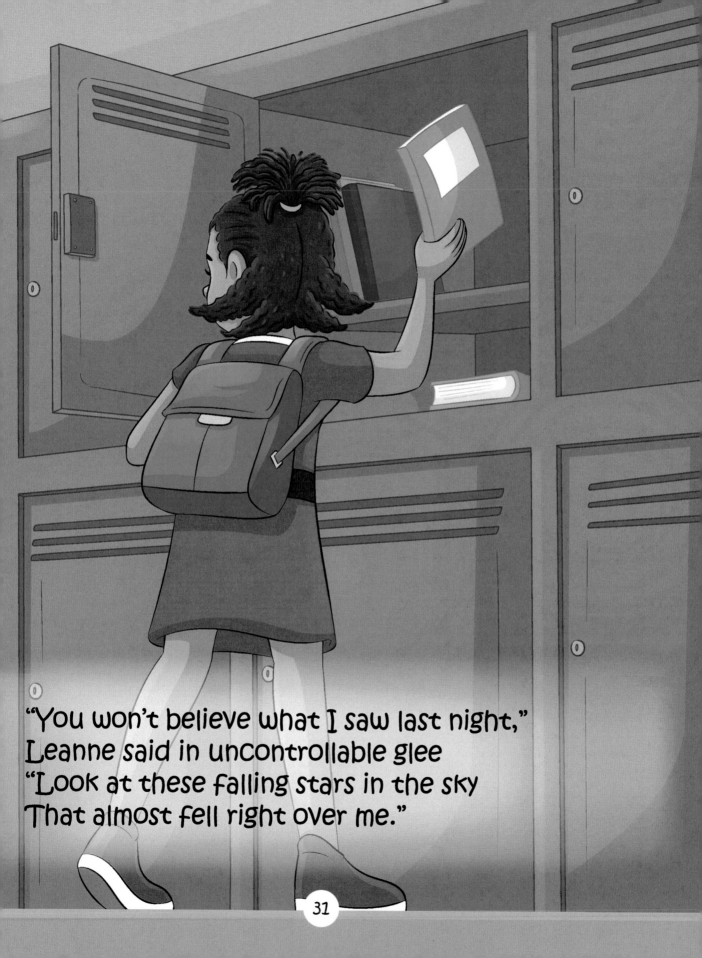

"You won't believe what I saw last night,"
Leanne said in uncontrollable glee
"Look at these falling stars in the sky
That almost fell right over me."

Ari watched in total disbelief
As Leanne continued to share
A red, a purple, and a pink ray of light
Rapidly shooting in the air.

Could what Ari thought was only a dream
Been something so much more?
Was her dream possibly a reality
Is what Ari planned to explore.

She couldn't wait to get home that night
And sleep while holding her sister's hands
To see if they could once again experience
A journey to another land.

But Ari and her sisters would have to wait
For their powers needed time to mature.
Their unique gifts were growing into something
That one day could not be stored.

For now, Ari took pleasure in knowing
That at least her sisters wouldn't be afraid
Of being in the dark together at night
Because nothing evil would ever invade.

Together they were a growing force
Of strength, wisdom, and beauty
That would one day take on the outside world
In a way no one would believe.

CHAPTER 2:
LISTEN AND LEARN

Have you ever found it hard to focus
When loud noises were too much to bare?
Well, Bri of the ElleRay sisters learned one day
How to channel the sounds of the air

It was after dinner
when Mommy checked over homework
And came across a note from Bri's teacher
It stated that Bri was not listening in class
And at times she was unable to reach her.

The teacher said that Bri seemed distracted
Sometimes sitting quietly, never making a sound
She suggested they see someone qualified
To help Bri focus more on the things around.

The next day Mommy took Bri
To the Special Doctor on the other side of town
The doctor evaluated Bri thoroughly
And told Mommy there was nothing he found.

"She hears everything just fine," he said.
"Sometimes she responds before I can say a word.
Her hearing and understanding are amazing
For someone so young is quite unheard."

Mommy thanked the doctor for taking the time
Then took Bri back to school the next day
Bri didn't want to miss the upcoming
school assembly
As her friends would be performing in a play.

Bri watched the assembly in amazement and awe
As she could hear them loud and clear
But when they lined up together to sing out loud
Bri had to cover her ears.

"What is wrong?" Mommy asked of Bri,
"Is everything ok?"
But the vibrations of noise that Bri could hear
Was just too much to say.

Bri ignored Mommy and kept her ears covered
For every performance thereafter
It was the only thing that Bri could do
To make sense of the noise and chatter.

Concerned that something was wrong with Bri
Mommy took her back home.
She needed to get Bri back to the Special Doctor
And immediately called him on the phone.

52

Bri started telling Ari and Little Lily
About all the things she heard
She talked nonstop about all the conversations
She told them word for word.

Mommy listened from the other room
As Bri described a number of sounds.
Then she heard Bri tell both Ari and Little Lily
About the vibrations that came from the ground.

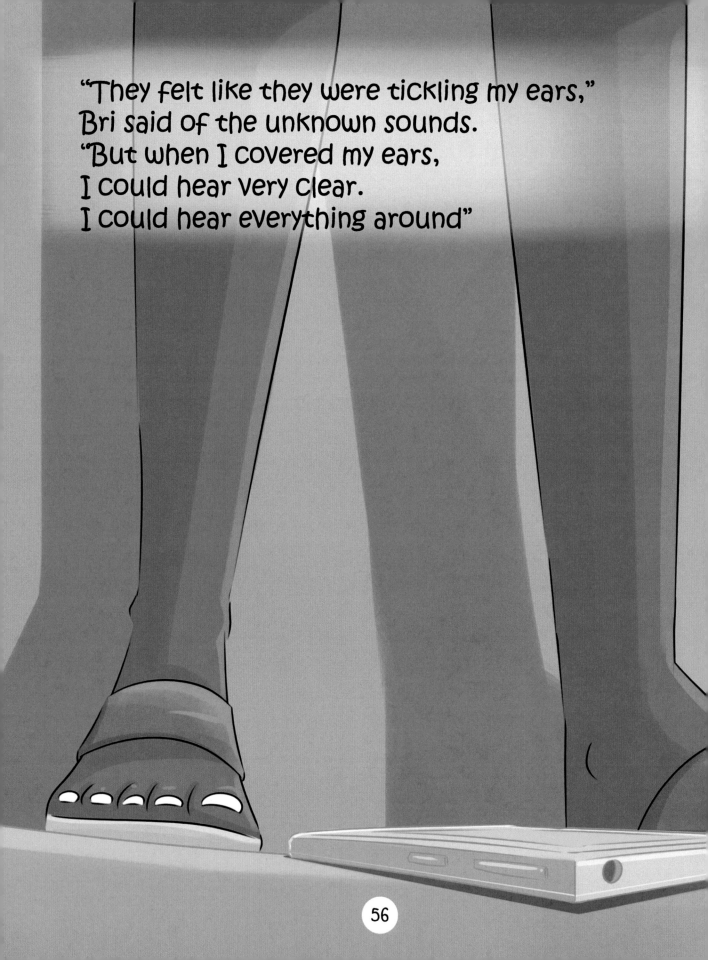

"They felt like they were tickling my ears,"
Bri said of the unknown sounds.
"But when I covered my ears,
I could hear very clear.
I could hear everything around"

Mommy dropped the phone in shock
She couldn't believe what Bri had said
Was Bri really telling her sisters that
She could hear what's inside someone's head?

Ari could hear things from a distance
And Bri could hear things unsaid.
Maybe this is just a phase Mommy thought
And so she sent the girls off to bed.

That night Mommy sat awake, unable to sleep
Thinking about what was going on with Bri.
She looked through her computer to find answers
But answers, she couldn't find any.

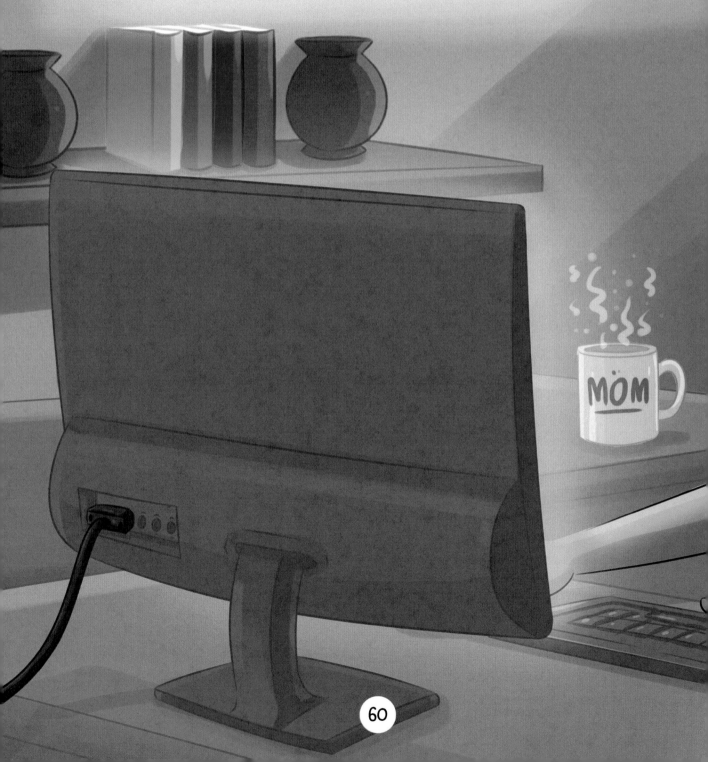

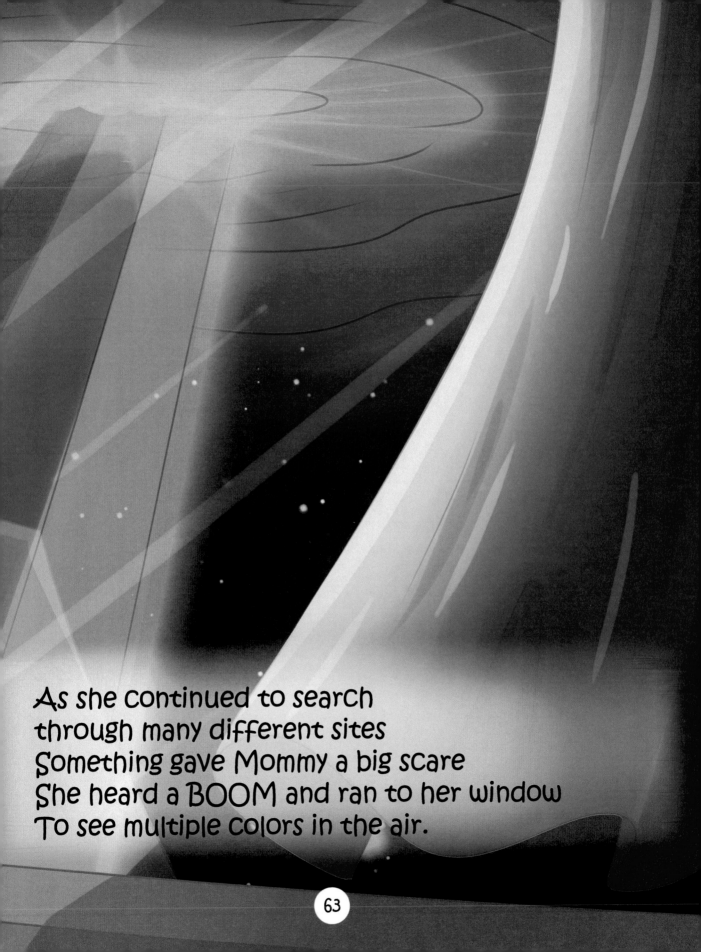

As she continued to search
through many different sites
Something gave Mommy a big scare
She heard a BOOM and ran to her window
To see multiple colors in the air.

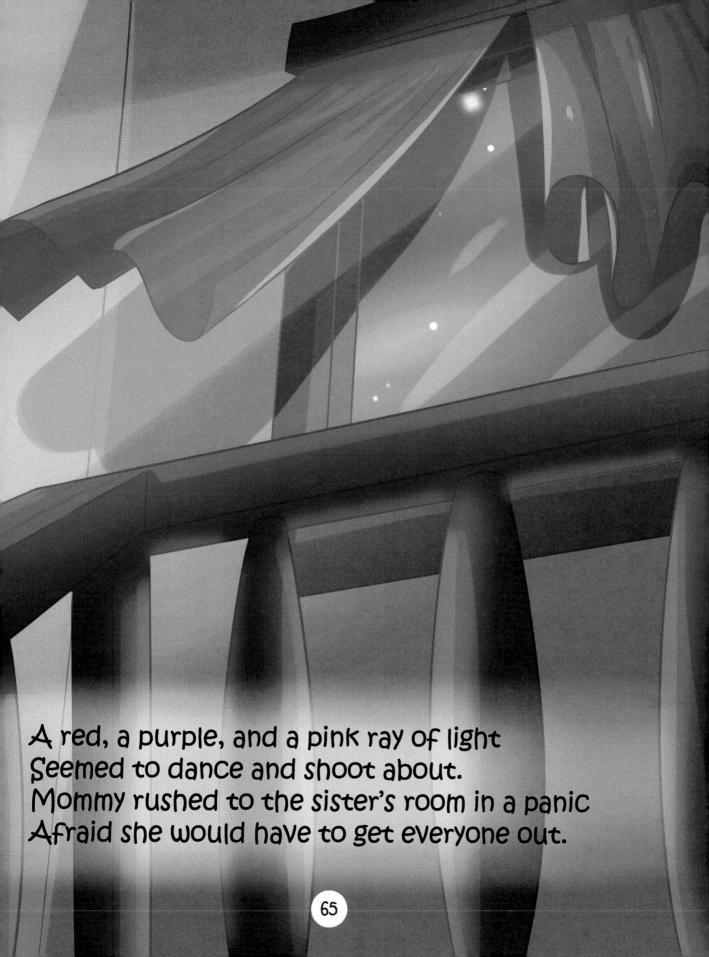

A red, a purple, and a pink ray of light
Seemed to dance and shoot about.
Mommy rushed to the sister's room in a panic
Afraid she would have to get everyone out.

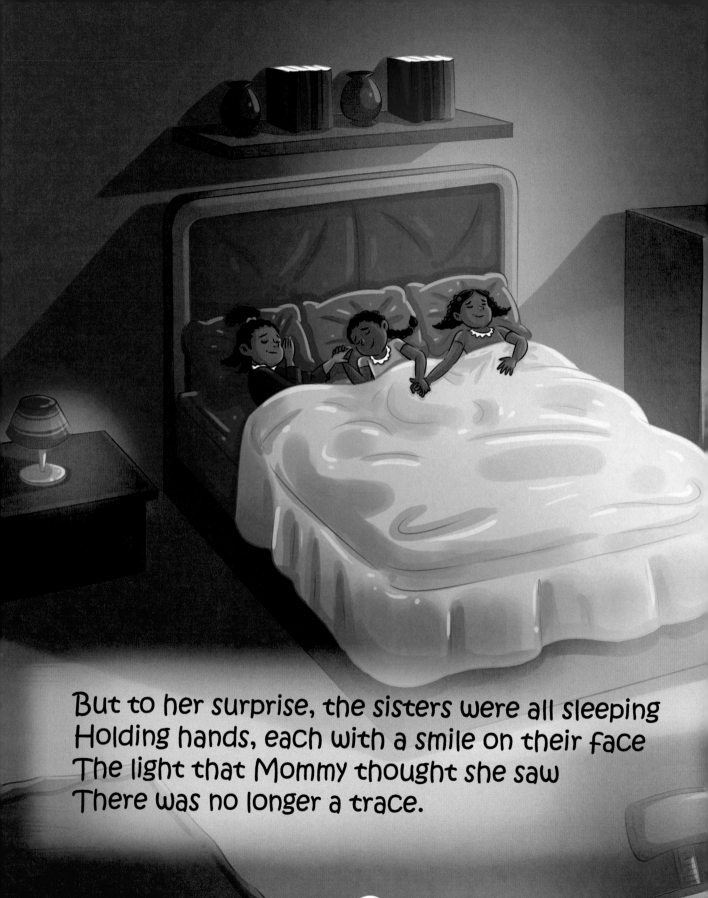

But to her surprise, the sisters were all sleeping
Holding hands, each with a smile on their face
The light that Mommy thought she saw
There was no longer a trace.

For now, Mommy would have to wait
And watch her daughters close
She thought she needed to protect them
from the world
But could it be the world needed
protection the most?

CHAPTER 3: DISCOVER THE UNKNOWN

Have you ever tried to say something
That you couldn't quite put into words?
Or maybe you had all the answers
But you just couldn't be heard.

Well, number three of the ElleRay sisters
Better known as Little Lily
Opened the last eye and unlocked all the answers
To the questions of things that
Mommy couldn't see.

The sisters were in the backyard with Mommy
Taking their time, planting eucalyptus trees.
But Little Lily was impatient and wanted it to grow
So she tried with her best ability.

"Grow, grow, grow," Little Lily said
While into the dirt Mommy continued to pound
Then Ari and Bri came over
And placed both of their hands into ground.

"Girls, don't do that! Go wash your hands!"
Mommy instructed to Ari and Bri
"I don't want you to bring more germs
into the house.
Now, go wash immediately."

With her back turned, Mommy couldn't see
What Little Lily was doing behind her.
But she, too, had placed her hands in the dirt
And the ground began to stir.

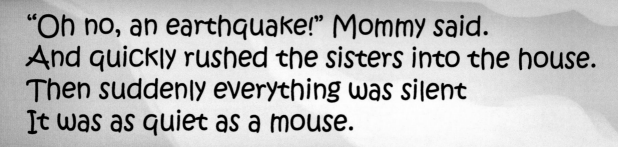

"Oh no, an earthquake!" Mommy said.
And quickly rushed the sisters into the house.
Then suddenly everything was silent
It was as quiet as a mouse.

"Girls, are you okay?" Mommy asked.
"I think we just had an earthquake."
"What about our trees?" Ari asked.
"I don't want any of them to break."

"It takes a while for trees to grow baby."
Mommy said to calm Ari down.
"I'm sure the trees will be just fine.
But for now, we need to go into town."

As they walked back out the door
Mommy dropped her purse in shock and disbelief
Because looming high above her
Were three eucalyptus trees.

Excited of their new discovery
Ari, Bri, and Little Lily joined hands
They did Ring Around the Rosie
In front of the new trees that were so grand.

But as they spun together in a circle
The sight of the sisters became a blur
They spun so fast and quickly
That all you could see was color after color.

Mommy remembered seeing this before
She remembered seeing the light
Of red, of purple, of pink tiny rays
Shooting through the sky the other night.

Then out of nowhere everything started to grow
In strength, in beauty, and in wisdom
Every plant was strong, every flower was colorful
And Mommy could now see with perfect vision

92

Her daughters had somehow unearthed a power
That allowed them to do marvelous things
But what else could they do she wondered
And what trouble would this bring?

The girls finally stopped spinning and looked in awe
At the array of trees and plants
Which they created by using their powers
And joining together their hands.

For now, Mommy thought that it would be best
To keep all of this a secret.
She didn't want anyone else to know
So, to herself, she would have to keep it.

Mommy gave them all a big hug
And thanked them for what they had done
What Mommy didn't know was that
their powers were still growing
And it had only just begun.